If your child struggles with a word, you can encourage "sounding it out," but keep in mind that not all words can be sounded out. Your child might pick up clues about a word from the picture, other words in the sentence, or any rhyming patterns. If your child struggles with a word for more than five seconds, it is usually best to simply say the word.

Most of all, remember to praise your child's efforts and keep the reading fun. After you have finished the book, ask a few questions and discuss what you have read together. Rereading this book multiple times may also be helpful for your child.

Try to keep the tips above in mind as you read together, but don't worry about doing everything right. Simply sharing the enjoyment of reading together will increase your child's reading skills and help to start your child off on a lifetime of reading enjoyment!

My Car Trip
A We Both Read® Book

With fond memories of all my family vacations . . .
—D. P.

Text Copyright © 2005 by Sindy McKay
Illustrations Copyright © 2005 by Meredith Johnson

We Both Read® is a registered trademark of Treasure Bay, Inc.

Published by
Treasure Bay, Inc.
P.O. Box 119
Novato, CA 94948 USA

Printed in Malaysia

Library of Congress Catalog Card Number: 2004115435

Hardcover ISBN: 978-1-891327-63-6
Paperback ISBN: 978-1-891327-64-3

We Both Read® Books
Patent No. 5,957,693

Visit us online at:
www.WeBothRead.com

11-15

My Car Trip

By Sindy McKay

Illustrated by Meredith Johnson

TREASURE BAY

We're taking a car trip. We're traveling far.

We're visiting Grandpa. We're driving the . . .

. . . car.

I love it at Grandpa's. It's never a bore.

He lives in the country and runs his own . . .

. . . store.

"Let's go!" calls my father. "We're all loaded up!"

I buckle my seat belt and so does my . . .

. . . pup.

My dad tells my mom she's in charge of the map. Then he turns on the engine and puts on his . . .

. . . cap.

We head for the highway, but then we get stuck.

Up ahead on the road is a broken down . . .

. . . truck.

We finally move and it's nice for a bit.

But all you can do is watch scenery and . . .

. . . sit.

I'm getting so bored! And the trip is so long!

Then Mom turns and says to me, "Let's sing . . .

. . . a song."

My mom knows a song that goes, "Are we there yet?"
My dad knows a song about flying . . .

. . . a jet.

The singing is fun and it helps the time pass.
Before we all know it, it's time to get . . .

. . . gas.

Then Dad says, "Who's hungry?" and I shout out, "Me!"
We drive to a café and park by . . .

. . . a tree.

I order a burger and big batch of fries.
Then I choose my dessert from a big tray of . . .

. . . pies.

My dog waits so patiently 'til we're all done.

I put on his leash and we go for . . .

. . . a run.

I take my dog back and he climbs in my lap.

While Dad keeps on driving, we both take . . .

. . . a nap.

👓 I dream about Grandpa, just waiting for me.
I dream of his store and the cool things I'll . . .

 . . . see.

Inside of his store there are fish poles and pails.

And lanterns and cook stoves and hammers . . .

. . . and nails.

There's dish soap and tissues and puzzles with words.

There's popcorn and apples and seed for . . .

. . . the birds.

There's even a rocking chair and an old trunk.

And stuff to wash up in, if you meet . . .

. . . a skunk.

My mom wakes me up and says, "Honey, we're here."
I look out the window and see a few . . .

. . . deer.

We pull up the driveway and now I can see,

that Grandpa is outside, just waiting for . . .

. . . me.

We've travelled all day and we're finally done.
The car trip was long, but it really was . . .

. . . fun.

If you liked *My Car Trip*, here are two other We Both Read® Books you are sure to enjoy!

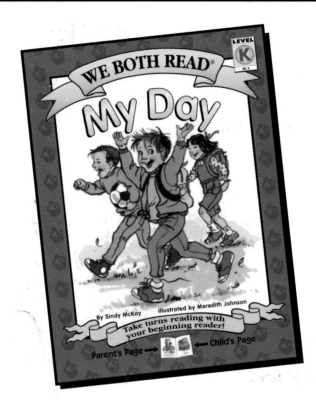

This Level K book is designed for the child who is just being introduced to reading. The child's pages have only one or two words, which relate directly to the illustration and even rhyme with what has just been read to them. This title is a charming story about what a child does in the course of a simple happy day.